NICU Journal FOR TRIPLETS

A 9 WEEK NEONATAL INTENSIVE CARE UNIT NOTEBOOK

HOW TO USE THIS BOOK

Included in this journal are nine weeks of tracking prompts to record the progress of your precious triplets during their NICU stay. You will begin the journey by introducing your little ones and sharing the events surrounding their entrance into the world. There's even pages to log your visitors.

Each day in the NICU consists of two pages with prompts and room for journaling. To help you organize your thoughts and the events that happen so quickly, there's a line for the date and a place to enter your babies' NICU day. Following every seven days, there are pages to summarize the week's progress, add additional information, photos, drawings or doodling. It will be rewarding to look back and remember their growth, daily activities, goals, struggles, and successes.

On the last few pages, you can document the events of the long awaited day when you take your bundles of joy home. There's also a place to keep track of items you need to remember and a shopping list page to ease the transition of going home.

Begin whenever you wish, and use this journal to suit your needs; there are no rules. You can even color the cute little woodland animals – if it will help you to relax.

Copyright 2019
Mellanie Kay Journals

Introducing

NAME

DATE OF BIRTH:

GESTATIONAL AGE:

TIME:

WEIGHT:

LENGTH:

HOSPITAL:

PROUD PARENTS:

MORE ABOUT MY BIRTHDAY:

Introducing

NAME

DATE OF BIRTH: _____

GESTATIONAL AGE: _____

TIME: _____

WEIGHT: _____

LENGTH: _____

HOSPITAL: _____

PROUD PARENTS: _____

MORE ABOUT MY BIRTHDAY: _____

_____

_____

_____

Introducing

NAME

DATE OF BIRTH:

GESTATIONAL AGE:

TIME:

WEIGHT:

LENGTH:

HOSPITAL:

PROUD PARENTS:

MORE ABOUT MY BIRTHDAY:

MAMA'S little MIRACLES

Visitors

DATE	NAME

Visitors

DATE	NAME

TODAY'S DATE: **NICU DAY #**

TODAY'S *Nurse*

TODAY'S *Doctor*

TODAY'S *Weather*

CURRENT *Events*

NOTES *& Reflections*

_____
_____
_____
_____
_____
_____

Milestones

_____
_____
_____
_____
_____

Positives

Hardships

Today... WE WERE BUSY!

___ FEEDING	___ READ	___ DIAPER
___ PHONE CALL	___ VIDEO CALL	___ ROCKED
___ SKIN ON SKIN	___ PRAYED	___ BATH
___ MASSAGE	___ TEMPERATURE	___ VISITORS

Feeding SCHEDULE

NAME	NAME	NAME

Goals FOR TODAY

Questions TO ASK

Today's STATS

 WEIGHT: LENGTH:

 GESTATIONAL AGE:

 LABS/MEDS/PROCEDURES:

 WEIGHT: LENGTH:

 GESTATIONAL AGE:

LABS/MEDS/PROCEDURES:

 WEIGHT: LENGTH:

 GESTATIONAL AGE:

 LABS/MEDS/PROCEDURES:

TODAY'S *Nurse*

NOTES & *Reflections*

_____
_____
_____
_____
_____

TODAY'S *Doctor*

_____
_____
_____
_____

TODAY'S *Weather*

Milestones

_____
_____

CURRENT *Events*

_____
_____
_____
_____

Positives

Hardships

Today... WE WERE BUSY!

FEEDING	READ	DIAPER
PHONE CALL	VIDEO CALL	ROCKED
SKIN ON SKIN	PRAYED	BATH
MASSAGE	TEMPERATURE	VISITORS

Feeding SCHEDULE

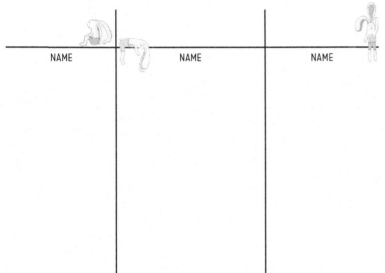

NAME   NAME   NAME

Goals FOR TODAY

Questions TO ASK

Today's STATS

 WEIGHT: LENGTH:

 GESTATIONAL AGE:

LABS/MEDS/PROCEDURES:

 WEIGHT: LENGTH:

 GESTATIONAL AGE:

LABS/MEDS/PROCEDURES:

 WEIGHT: LENGTH:

 GESTATIONAL AGE:

 LABS/MEDS/PROCEDURES:

TODAY'S *Nurse*

TODAY'S *Doctor*

TODAY'S *Weather*

CURRENT *Events*

NOTES & *Reflections*

Milestones

Positives

Hardships

Today... WE WERE BUSY!

___ FEEDING	___ READ	___ DIAPER
___ PHONE CALL	___ VIDEO CALL	___ ROCKED
___ SKIN ON SKIN	___ PRAYED	___ BATH
___ MASSAGE	___ TEMPERATURE	___ VISITORS

Feeding SCHEDULE

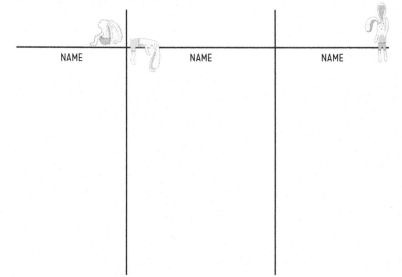

NAME   NAME   NAME

Goals FOR TODAY

Questions TO ASK

Today's STATS

 WEIGHT: LENGTH:

 GESTATIONAL AGE:

 LABS/MEDS/PROCEDURES:

 WEIGHT: LENGTH:

 GESTATIONAL AGE:

LABS/MEDS/PROCEDURES:

 WEIGHT: LENGTH:

 GESTATIONAL AGE:

 LABS/MEDS/PROCEDURES:

TODAY'S DATE:

NICU DAY #

TODAY'S *Nurse*

NOTES *& Reflections*

TODAY'S *Doctor*

TODAY'S *Weather*

Milestones

CURRENT *Events*

Positives

Hardships

Today... WE WERE BUSY!

FEEDING	READ	DIAPER
PHONE CALL	VIDEO CALL	ROCKED
SKIN ON SKIN	PRAYED	BATH
MASSAGE	TEMPERATURE	VISITORS

Feeding SCHEDULE

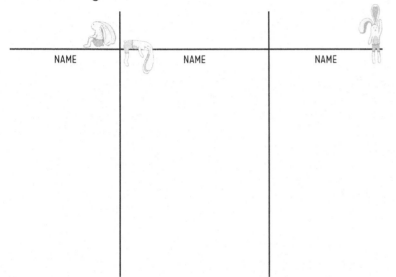

NAME   NAME   NAME

Goals FOR TODAY

Questions TO ASK

Today's STATS

 WEIGHT: LENGTH:

 GESTATIONAL AGE:

LABS/MEDS/PROCEDURES:

 WEIGHT: LENGTH:

 GESTATIONAL AGE:

LABS/MEDS/PROCEDURES:

 WEIGHT: LENGTH:

 GESTATIONAL AGE:

 LABS/MEDS/PROCEDURES:

TODAY'S DATE: **NICU DAY #**

TODAY'S *Nurse*

TODAY'S *Doctor*

TODAY'S *Weather*

CURRENT *Events*

NOTES *& Reflections*

_____
_____
_____
_____
_____
_____

Milestones

_____
_____
_____
_____

Positives

Hardships

Today... WE WERE BUSY!

FEEDING	READ	DIAPER
PHONE CALL	VIDEO CALL	ROCKED
SKIN ON SKIN	PRAYED	BATH
MASSAGE	TEMPERATURE	VISITORS

Feeding SCHEDULE

NAME	NAME	NAME

Goals FOR TODAY

Questions TO ASK

Today's STATS

 WEIGHT: LENGTH:

 GESTATIONAL AGE:

LABS/MEDS/PROCEDURES:

 WEIGHT: LENGTH:

 GESTATIONAL AGE:

 LABS/MEDS/PROCEDURES:

 WEIGHT: LENGTH:

 GESTATIONAL AGE:

 LABS/MEDS/PROCEDURES:

TODAY'S DATE: **NICU DAY #**

TODAY'S *Nurse*

TODAY'S *Doctor*

TODAY'S *Weather*

CURRENT *Events*

NOTES *& Reflections*

Milestones

Positives

Hardships

Today... WE WERE BUSY!

_____ FEEDING	_____ READ	_____ DIAPER
_____ PHONE CALL	_____ VIDEO CALL	_____ ROCKED
_____ SKIN ON SKIN	_____ PRAYED	_____ BATH
_____ MASSAGE	_____ TEMPERATURE	_____ VISITORS

Feeding SCHEDULE

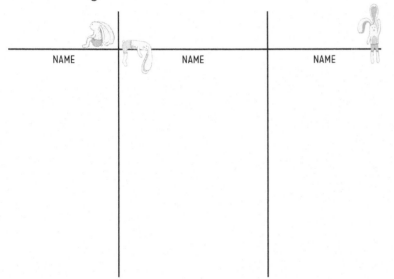

NAME	NAME	NAME

Goals FOR TODAY

Questions TO ASK

Today's STATS

 WEIGHT: LENGTH:

 GESTATIONAL AGE:

LABS/MEDS/PROCEDURES:

 WEIGHT: LENGTH:

 GESTATIONAL AGE:

LABS/MEDS/PROCEDURES:

 WEIGHT: LENGTH:

 GESTATIONAL AGE:

 LABS/MEDS/PROCEDURES:

TODAY'S DATE: **NICU DAY #**

TODAY'S *Nurse*

TODAY'S *Doctor*

TODAY'S *Weather*

CURRENT *Events*

NOTES *& Reflections*

_____
_____
_____
_____
_____
_____

Milestones

_____
_____
_____
_____
_____

Positives

Hardships

Today... WE WERE BUSY!

FEEDING	READ	DIAPER
PHONE CALL	VIDEO CALL	ROCKED
SKIN ON SKIN	PRAYED	BATH
MASSAGE	TEMPERATURE	VISITORS

Feeding SCHEDULE

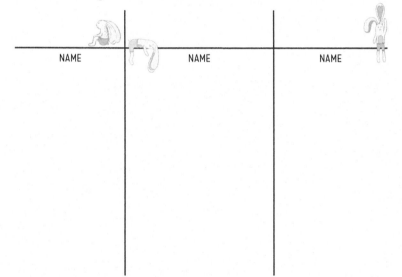

NAME	NAME	NAME

Goals FOR TODAY

Questions TO ASK

Today's STATS

 WEIGHT: LENGTH:

 GESTATIONAL AGE:

 LABS/MEDS/PROCEDURES:

 WEIGHT: LENGTH:

 GESTATIONAL AGE:

LABS/MEDS/PROCEDURES:

 WEIGHT: LENGTH:

 GESTATIONAL AGE:

 LABS/MEDS/PROCEDURES:

Photos

Weekly Recap

_____
_____
_____
_____
_____
_____
_____

TODAY'S DATE: NICU DAY #

TODAY'S *Nurse*

NOTES *& Reflections*

TODAY'S *Doctor*

_____

_____

_____

TODAY'S *Weather*

_____

Milestones

_____

_____

CURRENT *Events*

_____

_____

_____

Positives

Hardships

Today... WE WERE BUSY!

FEEDING	READ	DIAPER
PHONE CALL	VIDEO CALL	ROCKED
SKIN ON SKIN	PRAYED	BATH
MASSAGE	TEMPERATURE	VISITORS

Feeding SCHEDULE

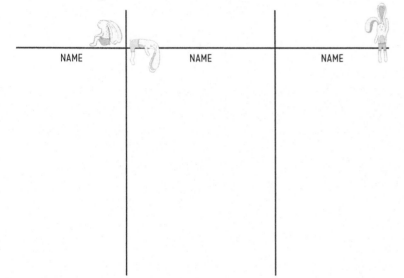

NAME	NAME	NAME

Goals FOR TODAY

Questions TO ASK

Today's STATS

 WEIGHT: LENGTH:

 GESTATIONAL AGE:

 LABS/MEDS/PROCEDURES:

 WEIGHT: LENGTH:

 GESTATIONAL AGE:

LABS/MEDS/PROCEDURES:

 WEIGHT: LENGTH:

 GESTATIONAL AGE:

 LABS/MEDS/PROCEDURES:

TODAY'S DATE: **NICU DAY #**

TODAY'S *Nurse*

NOTES *& Reflections*

_____
_____
_____
_____
_____
_____

TODAY'S *Doctor*

TODAY'S *Weather*

Milestones

_____
_____

CURRENT *Events*

_____
_____
_____

Positives

Hardships

Today... WE WERE BUSY!

FEEDING   READ   DIAPER

PHONE CALL   VIDEO CALL   ROCKED

SKIN ON SKIN   PRAYED   BATH

MASSAGE   TEMPERATURE   VISITORS

Feeding SCHEDULE

NAME	NAME	NAME

Goals FOR TODAY

Questions TO ASK

Today's STATS

 WEIGHT: LENGTH:

 GESTATIONAL AGE:

 LABS/MEDS/PROCEDURES:

 WEIGHT: LENGTH:

 GESTATIONAL AGE:

LABS/MEDS/PROCEDURES:

 WEIGHT: LENGTH:

 GESTATIONAL AGE:

 LABS/MEDS/PROCEDURES:

TODAY'S DATE: **NICU DAY #**

TODAY'S *Nurse*

TODAY'S *Doctor*

TODAY'S *Weather*

CURRENT *Events*

NOTES & *Reflections*

_____
_____
_____
_____
_____
_____
_____

Milestones

_____
_____
_____
_____
_____

Positives   *Hardships*

Today... WE WERE BUSY!

FEEDING   READ   DIAPER

PHONE CALL   VIDEO CALL   ROCKED

SKIN ON SKIN   PRAYED   BATH

MASSAGE   TEMPERATURE   VISITORS

Feeding SCHEDULE

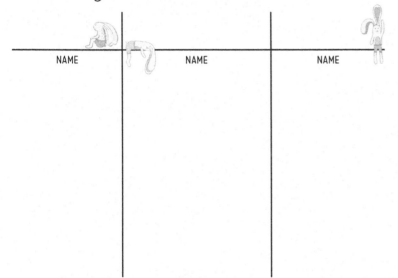

NAME   NAME   NAME

Goals FOR TODAY

Questions TO ASK

Today's STATS

 WEIGHT: LENGTH:

 GESTATIONAL AGE:

 LABS/MEDS/PROCEDURES:

 WEIGHT: LENGTH:

 GESTATIONAL AGE:

LABS/MEDS/PROCEDURES:

 WEIGHT: LENGTH:

 GESTATIONAL AGE:

 LABS/MEDS/PROCEDURES:

TODAY'S *Nurse*

NOTES *& Reflections*

_____
_____
_____

TODAY'S *Doctor*

_____
_____
_____

TODAY'S *Weather*

_____
_____

Milestones

_____
_____

CURRENT *Events*

_____
_____
_____

Positives

Hardships

Today... WE WERE BUSY!

FEEDING	READ	DIAPER
PHONE CALL	VIDEO CALL	ROCKED
SKIN ON SKIN	PRAYED	BATH
MASSAGE	TEMPERATURE	VISITORS

Feeding SCHEDULE

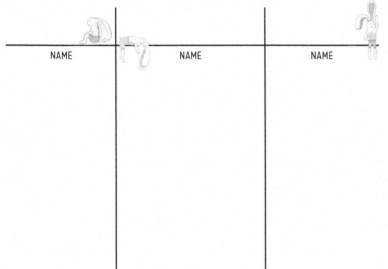

NAME	NAME	NAME

Goals FOR TODAY

Questions TO ASK

Today's STATS

 WEIGHT: LENGTH:

 GESTATIONAL AGE:

LABS/MEDS/PROCEDURES:

 WEIGHT: LENGTH:

 GESTATIONAL AGE:

 LABS/MEDS/PROCEDURES:

 WEIGHT: LENGTH:

 GESTATIONAL AGE:

 LABS/MEDS/PROCEDURES:

TODAY'S *Nurse*

NOTES *& Reflections*

TODAY'S *Doctor*

TODAY'S *Weather*

Milestones

CURRENT *Events*

Positives   *Hardships*

Today... WE WERE BUSY!

FEEDING	READ	DIAPER
PHONE CALL	VIDEO CALL	ROCKED
SKIN ON SKIN	PRAYED	BATH
MASSAGE	TEMPERATURE	VISITORS

Feeding SCHEDULE

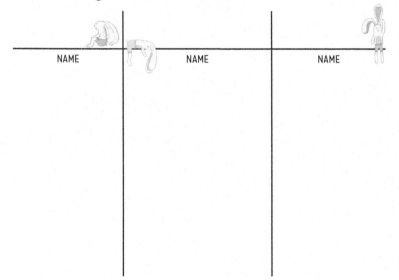

NAME   NAME   NAME

Goals FOR TODAY

Questions TO ASK

Today's STATS

 WEIGHT: LENGTH:

 GESTATIONAL AGE:

LABS/MEDS/PROCEDURES:

 WEIGHT: LENGTH:

 GESTATIONAL AGE:

 LABS/MEDS/PROCEDURES:

 WEIGHT: LENGTH:

 GESTATIONAL AGE:

 LABS/MEDS/PROCEDURES:

TODAY'S DATE: **NICU DAY #**

TODAY'S *Nurse*

TODAY'S *Doctor*

TODAY'S *Weather*

CURRENT *Events*

NOTES *& Reflections*

_____
_____
_____
_____
_____
_____

Milestones

_____
_____
_____
_____
_____

Positives

Hardships

Today... WE WERE BUSY!

FEEDING   READ   DIAPER

PHONE CALL   VIDEO CALL   ROCKED

SKIN ON SKIN   PRAYED   BATH

MASSAGE   TEMPERATURE   VISITORS

Feeding SCHEDULE

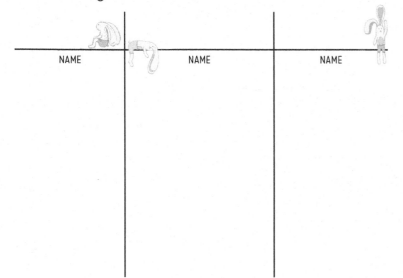

NAME	NAME	NAME

Goals FOR TODAY

Questions TO ASK

Today's STATS

 WEIGHT: LENGTH:

 GESTATIONAL AGE:

 LABS/MEDS/PROCEDURES:

 WEIGHT: LENGTH:

 GESTATIONAL AGE:

LABS/MEDS/PROCEDURES:

 WEIGHT: LENGTH:

 GESTATIONAL AGE:

 LABS/MEDS/PROCEDURES:

TODAY'S DATE: **NICU DAY #**

TODAY'S *Nurse*

TODAY'S *Doctor*

TODAY'S *Weather*

CURRENT *Events*

NOTES *& Reflections*

Milestones

Positives

Hardships

Today... WE WERE BUSY!

FEEDING	READ	DIAPER
PHONE CALL	VIDEO CALL	ROCKED
SKIN ON SKIN	PRAYED	BATH
MASSAGE	TEMPERATURE	VISITORS

Feeding SCHEDULE

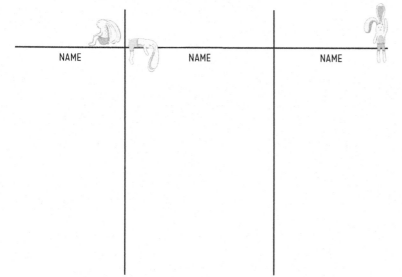

NAME   NAME   NAME

Goals FOR TODAY

Questions TO ASK

Today's STATS

 WEIGHT: LENGTH:

 GESTATIONAL AGE:

 LABS/MEDS/PROCEDURES:

 WEIGHT: LENGTH:

 GESTATIONAL AGE:

LABS/MEDS/PROCEDURES:

 WEIGHT: LENGTH:

 GESTATIONAL AGE:

 LABS/MEDS/PROCEDURES:

Photos

Weekly Recap

_____

_____

_____

_____

_____

_____

_____

_____

TODAY'S DATE: **NICU DAY #**

TODAY'S *Nurse*

TODAY'S *Doctor*

TODAY'S *Weather*

CURRENT *Events*

NOTES *& Reflections*

_____
_____
_____
_____
_____
_____

Milestones

_____
_____
_____
_____

Positives

Hardships

Today... WE WERE BUSY!

FEEDING   READ   DIAPER

PHONE CALL   VIDEO CALL   ROCKED

SKIN ON SKIN   PRAYED   BATH

MASSAGE   TEMPERATURE   VISITORS

Feeding SCHEDULE

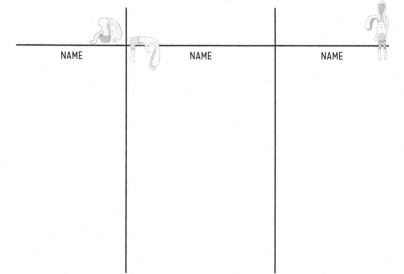

NAME   NAME   NAME

Goals FOR TODAY

Questions TO ASK

 WEIGHT: LENGTH:

 GESTATIONAL AGE:

 LABS/MEDS/PROCEDURES:

WEIGHT: LENGTH:

GESTATIONAL AGE:

 LABS/MEDS/PROCEDURES:

 WEIGHT: LENGTH:

 GESTATIONAL AGE:

 LABS/MEDS/PROCEDURES:

TODAY'S DATE:

NICU DAY #

TODAY'S *Nurse*

TODAY'S *Doctor*

TODAY'S *Weather*

CURRENT *Events*

NOTES *& Reflections*

Milestones

Positives

Hardships

Today... WE WERE BUSY!

FEEDING _____   READ _____   DIAPER _____

PHONE CALL _____   VIDEO CALL _____   ROCKED _____

SKIN ON SKIN _____   PRAYED _____   BATH _____

MASSAGE _____   TEMPERATURE _____   VISITORS _____

Feeding SCHEDULE

NAME	NAME	NAME

Goals FOR TODAY

Questions TO ASK

Today's STATS

 WEIGHT: _____   LENGTH: _____

GESTATIONAL AGE:

LABS/MEDS/PROCEDURES:

 WEIGHT: _____   LENGTH: _____

GESTATIONAL AGE:

LABS/MEDS/PROCEDURES:

 WEIGHT: _____   LENGTH: _____

GESTATIONAL AGE:

LABS/MEDS/PROCEDURES:

TODAY'S DATE: **NICU DAY #**

TODAY'S *Nurse*

TODAY'S *Doctor*

TODAY'S *Weather*

CURRENT *Events*

NOTES *& Reflections*

Milestones

Positives

Hardships

Today... WE WERE BUSY!

FEEDING	READ	DIAPER
PHONE CALL	VIDEO CALL	ROCKED
SKIN ON SKIN	PRAYED	BATH
MASSAGE	TEMPERATURE	VISITORS

Feeding SCHEDULE

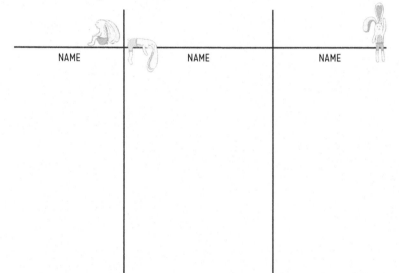

NAME	NAME	NAME

Goals FOR TODAY

Questions TO ASK

Today's STATS

 WEIGHT: LENGTH:

 GESTATIONAL AGE:

 LABS/MEDS/PROCEDURES:

 WEIGHT: LENGTH:

 GESTATIONAL AGE:

 LABS/MEDS/PROCEDURES:

 WEIGHT: LENGTH:

 GESTATIONAL AGE:

LABS/MEDS/PROCEDURES:

TODAY'S *Nurse*

TODAY'S *Doctor*

TODAY'S *Weather*

CURRENT *Events*

NOTES *& Reflections*

Milestones

Positives

Hardships

Today... WE WERE BUSY!

FEEDING	READ	DIAPER
PHONE CALL	VIDEO CALL	ROCKED
SKIN ON SKIN	PRAYED	BATH
MASSAGE	TEMPERATURE	VISITORS

Feeding SCHEDULE

NAME   NAME   NAME

Goals FOR TODAY

Questions TO ASK

Today's STATS

 WEIGHT: LENGTH:

 GESTATIONAL AGE:

LABS/MEDS/PROCEDURES:

 WEIGHT: LENGTH:

 GESTATIONAL AGE:

LABS/MEDS/PROCEDURES:

 WEIGHT: LENGTH:

 GESTATIONAL AGE:

 LABS/MEDS/PROCEDURES:

TODAY'S *Nurse*

NOTES *& Reflections*

_____
_____
_____
_____
_____

TODAY'S *Doctor*

_____
_____
_____

TODAY'S *Weather*

_____

Milestones

_____
_____

CURRENT *Events*

_____
_____
_____

Positives

Hardships

Today... WE WERE BUSY!

___ FEEDING	___ READ	___ DIAPER
___ PHONE CALL	___ VIDEO CALL	___ ROCKED
___ SKIN ON SKIN	___ PRAYED	___ BATH
___ MASSAGE	___ TEMPERATURE	___ VISITORS

Feeding SCHEDULE

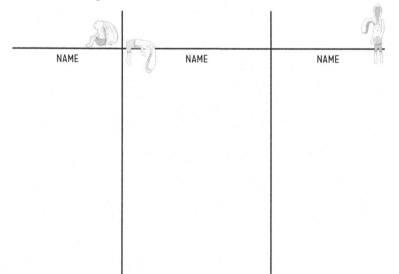

NAME	NAME	NAME

Goals FOR TODAY

Questions TO ASK

Today's STATS

 WEIGHT: LENGTH:

 GESTATIONAL AGE:

 LABS/MEDS/PROCEDURES:

 WEIGHT: LENGTH:

 GESTATIONAL AGE:

LABS/MEDS/PROCEDURES:

 WEIGHT: LENGTH:

 GESTATIONAL AGE:

 LABS/MEDS/PROCEDURES:

TODAY'S DATE: **NICU DAY #**

TODAY'S *Nurse*

TODAY'S *Doctor*

TODAY'S *Weather*

CURRENT *Events*

NOTES *& Reflections*

_____
_____
_____
_____
_____
_____

Milestones

_____
_____
_____
_____
_____

Positives

Hardships

Today... WE WERE BUSY!

FEEDING
PHONE CALL
SKIN ON SKIN
MASSAGE

READ
VIDEO CALL
PRAYED
TEMPERATURE

DIAPER
ROCKED
BATH
VISITORS

Feeding SCHEDULE

NAME	NAME	NAME

Goals FOR TODAY

Questions TO ASK

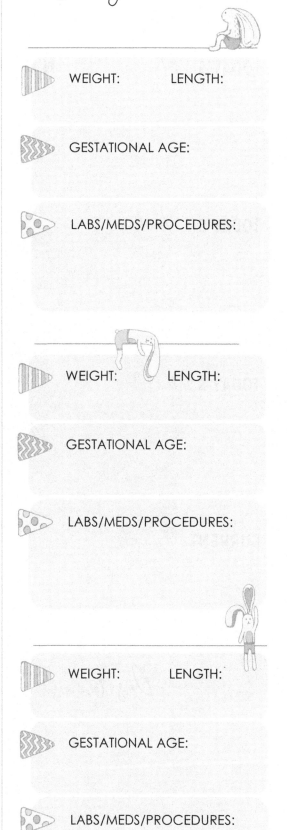

Today's STATS

WEIGHT: LENGTH:

GESTATIONAL AGE:

LABS/MEDS/PROCEDURES:

WEIGHT: LENGTH:

GESTATIONAL AGE:

LABS/MEDS/PROCEDURES:

WEIGHT: LENGTH:

GESTATIONAL AGE:

LABS/MEDS/PROCEDURES:

TODAY'S DATE:
NICU DAY #

TODAY'S *Nurse*

NOTES *& Reflections*

_____
_____
_____
_____
_____
_____
_____

TODAY'S *Doctor*

TODAY'S *Weather*

Milestones

_____
_____
_____

CURRENT *Events*

_____
_____
_____

Positives

Hardships

Today... WE WERE BUSY!

___ FEEDING	___ READ	___ DIAPER
___ PHONE CALL	___ VIDEO CALL	___ ROCKED
___ SKIN ON SKIN	___ PRAYED	___ BATH
___ MASSAGE	___ TEMPERATURE	___ VISITORS

Feeding SCHEDULE

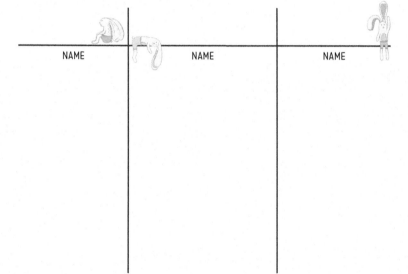

NAME   NAME   NAME

Goals FOR TODAY

Questions TO ASK

Today's STATS

 WEIGHT: LENGTH:

 GESTATIONAL AGE:

 LABS/MEDS/PROCEDURES:

 WEIGHT: LENGTH:

 GESTATIONAL AGE:

LABS/MEDS/PROCEDURES:

 WEIGHT: LENGTH:

 GESTATIONAL AGE:

 LABS/MEDS/PROCEDURES:

Photos

Weekly Recap

_____
_____
_____
_____
_____
_____
_____
_____

TODAY'S DATE:　　　　　　　　**NICU DAY #**

TODAY'S *Nurse*

TODAY'S *Doctor*

TODAY'S *Weather*

CURRENT *Events*

NOTES *& Reflections*

_____
_____
_____
_____
_____
_____
_____

Milestones

_____
_____
_____
_____
_____

Positives

Hardships

Today... WE WERE BUSY!

___ FEEDING	___ READ	___ DIAPER
___ PHONE CALL	___ VIDEO CALL	___ ROCKED
___ SKIN ON SKIN	___ PRAYED	___ BATH
___ MASSAGE	___ TEMPERATURE	___ VISITORS

Feeding SCHEDULE

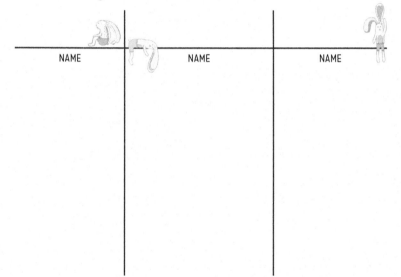

NAME   NAME   NAME

Goals FOR TODAY

Questions TO ASK

Today's STATS

 WEIGHT: LENGTH:

 GESTATIONAL AGE:

LABS/MEDS/PROCEDURES:

 WEIGHT: LENGTH:

 GESTATIONAL AGE:

 LABS/MEDS/PROCEDURES:

 WEIGHT: LENGTH:

 GESTATIONAL AGE:

 LABS/MEDS/PROCEDURES:

TODAY'S *Nurse*

NOTES *& Reflections*

_____
_____
_____

TODAY'S *Doctor*

_____
_____
_____
_____

TODAY'S *Weather*

_____

Milestones

_____
_____

CURRENT *Events*

_____
_____
_____
_____

Positives

Hardships

Today... WE WERE BUSY!

FEEDING	READ	DIAPER
PHONE CALL	VIDEO CALL	ROCKED
SKIN ON SKIN	PRAYED	BATH
MASSAGE	TEMPERATURE	VISITORS

Feeding SCHEDULE

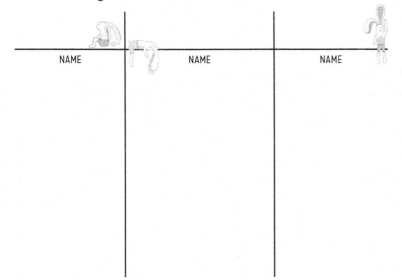

NAME   NAME   NAME

Goals FOR TODAY

Questions TO ASK

Today's STATS

 WEIGHT: LENGTH:

 GESTATIONAL AGE:

 LABS/MEDS/PROCEDURES:

 WEIGHT: LENGTH:

GESTATIONAL AGE:

 LABS/MEDS/PROCEDURES:

 WEIGHT: LENGTH:

 GESTATIONAL AGE:

 LABS/MEDS/PROCEDURES:

TODAY'S *Nurse*

NOTES & *Reflections*

_____

_____

_____

TODAY'S *Doctor*

_____

_____

_____

TODAY'S *Weather*

_____

Milestones

_____

_____

CURRENT *Events*

_____

_____

_____

Positives

Hardships

Today... WE WERE BUSY!

_____ FEEDING	_____ READ	_____ DIAPER
_____ PHONE CALL	_____ VIDEO CALL	_____ ROCKED
_____ SKIN ON SKIN	_____ PRAYED	_____ BATH
_____ MASSAGE	_____ TEMPERATURE	_____ VISITORS

Feeding SCHEDULE

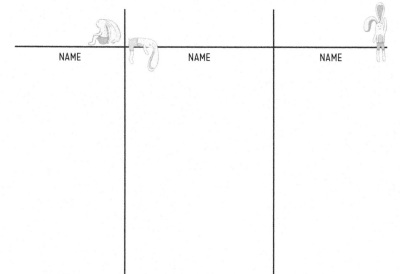

NAME	NAME	NAME

Goals FOR TODAY

Questions TO ASK

Today's STATS

 WEIGHT: _____ LENGTH:

 GESTATIONAL AGE:

LABS/MEDS/PROCEDURES:

 WEIGHT: _____ LENGTH:

 GESTATIONAL AGE:

 LABS/MEDS/PROCEDURES:

 WEIGHT: _____ LENGTH:

 GESTATIONAL AGE:

 LABS/MEDS/PROCEDURES:

TODAY'S *Nurse*

TODAY'S *Doctor*

TODAY'S *Weather*

CURRENT *Events*

NOTES *& Reflections*

Milestones

Positives

Hardships

Today... WE WERE BUSY!

FEEDING ____

READ ____

DIAPER ____

PHONE CALL ____

VIDEO CALL ____

ROCKED ____

SKIN ON SKIN ____

PRAYED ____

BATH ____

MASSAGE ____

TEMPERATURE ____

VISITORS ____

____

Feeding SCHEDULE

NAME	NAME	NAME

Goals FOR TODAY

Questions TO ASK

Today's STATS

_____

 WEIGHT: LENGTH:

 GESTATIONAL AGE:

 LABS/MEDS/PROCEDURES:

_____

 WEIGHT: LENGTH:

 GESTATIONAL AGE:

 LABS/MEDS/PROCEDURES:

_____

WEIGHT: LENGTH:

GESTATIONAL AGE:

 LABS/MEDS/PROCEDURES:

TODAY'S *Nurse*

TODAY'S *Doctor*

TODAY'S *Weather*

CURRENT *Events*

NOTES & *Reflections*

Milestones

Positives

Hardships

Today... WE WERE BUSY!

FEEDING ___

PHONE CALL ___

SKIN ON SKIN ___

MASSAGE ___

READ ___

VIDEO CALL ___

PRAYED ___

TEMPERATURE ___

DIAPER ___

ROCKED ___

BATH ___

VISITORS ___

Feeding SCHEDULE

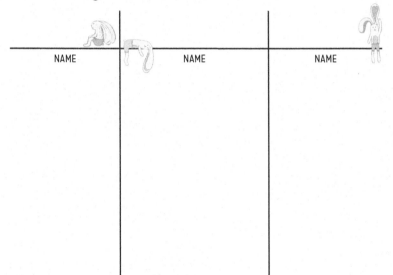

NAME	NAME	NAME

Goals FOR TODAY

Questions TO ASK

Today's STATS

 WEIGHT: _____ LENGTH: _____

 GESTATIONAL AGE: _____

 LABS/MEDS/PROCEDURES: _____

 WEIGHT: _____ LENGTH: _____

 GESTATIONAL AGE: _____

LABS/MEDS/PROCEDURES: _____

 WEIGHT: _____ LENGTH: _____

 GESTATIONAL AGE: _____

 LABS/MEDS/PROCEDURES: _____

TODAY'S *Nurse*

NOTES *& Reflections*

_____
_____
_____
_____
_____
_____

TODAY'S *Doctor*

_____
_____

TODAY'S *Weather*

Milestones

_____
_____

CURRENT *Events*

_____
_____
_____
_____

Positives

Hardships

Today... WE WERE BUSY!

___ FEEDING	___ READ	___ DIAPER
___ PHONE CALL	___ VIDEO CALL	___ ROCKED
___ SKIN ON SKIN	___ PRAYED	___ BATH
___ MASSAGE	___ TEMPERATURE	___ VISITORS

___

Feeding SCHEDULE

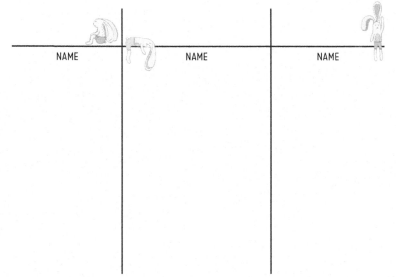

NAME   NAME   NAME

Goals FOR TODAY

Questions TO ASK

Today's STATS

 WEIGHT: LENGTH:

 GESTATIONAL AGE:

 LABS/MEDS/PROCEDURES:

 WEIGHT: LENGTH:

 GESTATIONAL AGE:

LABS/MEDS/PROCEDURES:

 WEIGHT: LENGTH:

 GESTATIONAL AGE:

 LABS/MEDS/PROCEDURES:

TODAY'S DATE: **NICU DAY #**

TODAY'S *Nurse*

TODAY'S *Doctor*

TODAY'S *Weather*

CURRENT *Events*

NOTES *& Reflections*

_____
_____
_____
_____
_____
_____

Milestones

_____
_____
_____
_____
_____

Positives

Hardships

Today... WE WERE BUSY!

FEEDING	READ	DIAPER
PHONE CALL	VIDEO CALL	ROCKED
SKIN ON SKIN	PRAYED	BATH
MASSAGE	TEMPERATURE	VISITORS

Feeding SCHEDULE

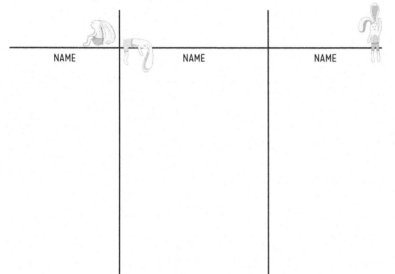

NAME   NAME   NAME

Goals FOR TODAY

Questions TO ASK

Today's STATS

 WEIGHT: LENGTH:

 GESTATIONAL AGE:

 LABS/MEDS/PROCEDURES:

 WEIGHT: LENGTH:

 GESTATIONAL AGE:

LABS/MEDS/PROCEDURES:

 WEIGHT: LENGTH:

 GESTATIONAL AGE:

 LABS/MEDS/PROCEDURES:

Photos

Weekly Recap

TODAY'S DATE: **NICU DAY #**

TODAY'S *Nurse*

NOTES *& Reflections*

TODAY'S *Doctor*

TODAY'S *Weather*

Milestones

CURRENT *Events*

Positives

Hardships

Today... WE WERE BUSY!

FEEDING	READ	DIAPER
PHONE CALL	VIDEO CALL	ROCKED
SKIN ON SKIN	PRAYED	BATH
MASSAGE	TEMPERATURE	VISITORS

Feeding SCHEDULE

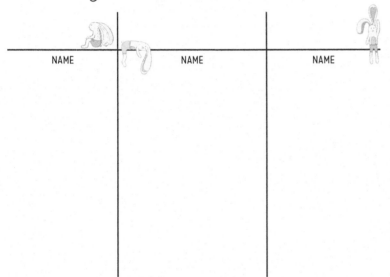

NAME   NAME   NAME

Goals FOR TODAY

Questions TO ASK

Today's STATS

 WEIGHT: LENGTH:

 GESTATIONAL AGE:

 LABS/MEDS/PROCEDURES:

 WEIGHT: LENGTH:

 GESTATIONAL AGE:

 LABS/MEDS/PROCEDURES:

 WEIGHT: LENGTH:

 GESTATIONAL AGE:

 LABS/MEDS/PROCEDURES:

TODAY'S DATE: **NICU DAY #**

TODAY'S *Nurse*

TODAY'S *Doctor*

TODAY'S *Weather*

CURRENT *Events*

NOTES *& Reflections*

Milestones

Positives

Hardships

Today... WE WERE BUSY!

FEEDING _____ READ _____ DIAPER _____

PHONE CALL _____ VIDEO CALL _____ ROCKED _____

SKIN ON SKIN _____ PRAYED _____ BATH _____

MASSAGE _____ TEMPERATURE _____ VISITORS _____

_____

Feeding SCHEDULE

NAME	NAME	NAME

Goals FOR TODAY

Questions TO ASK

Today's STATS

_____

WEIGHT: LENGTH:

GESTATIONAL AGE:

LABS/MEDS/PROCEDURES:

_____

WEIGHT: LENGTH:

GESTATIONAL AGE:

LABS/MEDS/PROCEDURES:

_____

WEIGHT: LENGTH:

GESTATIONAL AGE:

LABS/MEDS/PROCEDURES:

TODAY'S DATE: **NICU DAY #**

TODAY'S *Nurse*

TODAY'S *Doctor*

TODAY'S *Weather*

CURRENT *Events*

NOTES *& Reflections*

Milestones

Positives

Hardships

Today... WE WERE BUSY!

FEEDING	READ	DIAPER
PHONE CALL	VIDEO CALL	ROCKED
SKIN ON SKIN	PRAYED	BATH
MASSAGE	TEMPERATURE	VISITORS

Feeding SCHEDULE

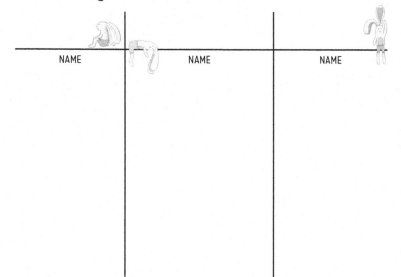

NAME   NAME   NAME

Goals FOR TODAY

Questions TO ASK

Today's STATS

 WEIGHT: LENGTH:

 GESTATIONAL AGE:

LABS/MEDS/PROCEDURES:

 WEIGHT: LENGTH:

 GESTATIONAL AGE:

 LABS/MEDS/PROCEDURES:

 WEIGHT: LENGTH:

 GESTATIONAL AGE:

 LABS/MEDS/PROCEDURES:

TODAY'S *Nurse*

TODAY'S *Doctor*

TODAY'S *Weather*

CURRENT *Events*

NOTES *& Reflections*

Milestones

Positives

Hardships

Today... WE WERE BUSY!

FEEDING
_____

PHONE CALL
_____

SKIN ON SKIN
_____

MASSAGE
_____

_____

READ
_____

VIDEO CALL
_____

PRAYED
_____

TEMPERATURE
_____

DIAPER
_____

ROCKED
_____

BATH
_____

VISITORS
_____

Feeding SCHEDULE

NAME	NAME	NAME

Goals FOR TODAY

Questions TO ASK

Today's STATS

 WEIGHT: LENGTH:

 GESTATIONAL AGE:

 LABS/MEDS/PROCEDURES:

 WEIGHT: LENGTH:

 GESTATIONAL AGE:

 LABS/MEDS/PROCEDURES:

 WEIGHT: LENGTH:

 GESTATIONAL AGE:

LABS/MEDS/PROCEDURES:

TODAY'S *Nurse*

TODAY'S *Doctor*

TODAY'S *Weather*

CURRENT *Events*

NOTES & *Reflections*

_____

_____

_____

_____

_____

_____

_____

Milestones

_____

_____

_____

_____

_____

Positives

Hardships

Today... WE WERE BUSY!

FEEDING	READ	DIAPER
PHONE CALL	VIDEO CALL	ROCKED
SKIN ON SKIN	PRAYED	BATH
MASSAGE	TEMPERATURE	VISITORS

Feeding SCHEDULE

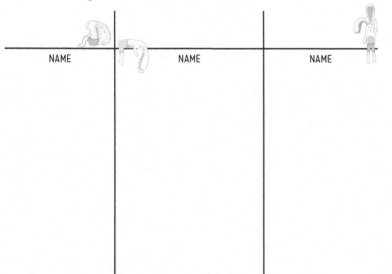

NAME	NAME	NAME

Goals FOR TODAY

Questions TO ASK

Today's STATS

 WEIGHT: LENGTH:

 GESTATIONAL AGE:

 LABS/MEDS/PROCEDURES:

 WEIGHT: LENGTH:

 GESTATIONAL AGE:

LABS/MEDS/PROCEDURES:

 WEIGHT: LENGTH:

 GESTATIONAL AGE:

 LABS/MEDS/PROCEDURES:

TODAY'S DATE: **NICU DAY #**

TODAY'S *Nurse*

NOTES *& Reflections*

TODAY'S *Doctor*

TODAY'S *Weather*

Milestones

CURRENT *Events*

Positives   *Hardships*

Today... WE WERE BUSY!

FEEDING	READ	DIAPER
PHONE CALL	VIDEO CALL	ROCKED
SKIN ON SKIN	PRAYED	BATH
MASSAGE	TEMPERATURE	VISITORS

Feeding SCHEDULE

NAME   NAME   NAME

Goals FOR TODAY

Questions TO ASK

Today's STATS

 WEIGHT: LENGTH:

 GESTATIONAL AGE:

 LABS/MEDS/PROCEDURES:

 WEIGHT: LENGTH:

 GESTATIONAL AGE:

LABS/MEDS/PROCEDURES:

 WEIGHT: LENGTH:

 GESTATIONAL AGE:

 LABS/MEDS/PROCEDURES:

TODAY'S DATE: **NICU DAY #**

TODAY'S *Nurse*

TODAY'S *Doctor*

TODAY'S *Weather*

CURRENT *Events*

NOTES *& Reflections*

_____
_____
_____
_____
_____
_____
_____

Milestones

_____
_____
_____
_____
_____

Positives

Hardships

Today... WE WERE BUSY!

FEEDING	READ	DIAPER
PHONE CALL	VIDEO CALL	ROCKED
SKIN ON SKIN	PRAYED	BATH
MASSAGE	TEMPERATURE	VISITORS

Feeding SCHEDULE

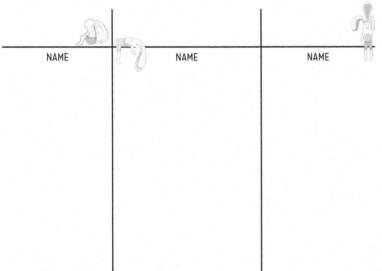

NAME   NAME   NAME

Goals FOR TODAY

Questions TO ASK

Today's STATS

 WEIGHT: LENGTH:

 GESTATIONAL AGE:

 LABS/MEDS/PROCEDURES:

 WEIGHT: LENGTH:

 GESTATIONAL AGE:

 LABS/MEDS/PROCEDURES:

 WEIGHT: LENGTH:

 GESTATIONAL AGE:

 LABS/MEDS/PROCEDURES:

Photos

Weekly Recap

_____
_____
_____
_____
_____
_____
_____

TODAY'S *Nurse*

TODAY'S *Doctor*

TODAY'S *Weather*

CURRENT *Events*

NOTES *& Reflections*

_____
_____
_____
_____
_____
_____

Milestones

_____
_____
_____
_____

Positives

Hardships

Today... WE WERE BUSY!

FEEDING

PHONE CALL

SKIN ON SKIN

MASSAGE

READ

VIDEO CALL

PRAYED

TEMPERATURE

DIAPER

ROCKED

BATH

VISITORS

Feeding SCHEDULE

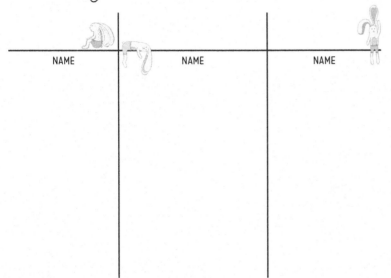

NAME	NAME	NAME

Goals FOR TODAY

Questions TO ASK

Today's STATS

 WEIGHT: LENGTH:

 GESTATIONAL AGE:

 LABS/MEDS/PROCEDURES:

 WEIGHT: LENGTH:

 GESTATIONAL AGE:

LABS/MEDS/PROCEDURES:

 WEIGHT: LENGTH:

 GESTATIONAL AGE:

 LABS/MEDS/PROCEDURES:

TODAY'S *Nurse*

TODAY'S *Doctor*

TODAY'S *Weather*

CURRENT *Events*

NOTES *& Reflections*

_____
_____
_____
_____
_____
_____
_____

Milestones

_____
_____
_____
_____
_____

Positives

Hardships

Today... WE WERE BUSY!

FEEDING   READ   DIAPER

PHONE CALL   VIDEO CALL   ROCKED

SKIN ON SKIN   PRAYED   BATH

MASSAGE   TEMPERATURE   VISITORS

Feeding SCHEDULE

NAME	NAME	NAME

Goals FOR TODAY

Questions TO ASK

Today's STATS

 WEIGHT: LENGTH:

 GESTATIONAL AGE:

 LABS/MEDS/PROCEDURES:

 WEIGHT: LENGTH:

 GESTATIONAL AGE:

LABS/MEDS/PROCEDURES:

 WEIGHT: LENGTH:

 GESTATIONAL AGE:

 LABS/MEDS/PROCEDURES:

TODAY'S DATE: NICU DAY #

TODAY'S *Nurse*

NOTES *& Reflections*

_____

_____

_____

TODAY'S *Doctor*

_____

_____

_____

_____

TODAY'S *Weather*

_____

Milestones

_____

_____

CURRENT *Events*

_____

_____

_____

Positives

Hardships

Today... WE WERE BUSY!

FEEDING

PHONE CALL

SKIN ON SKIN

MASSAGE

READ

VIDEO CALL

PRAYED

TEMPERATURE

DIAPER

ROCKED

BATH

VISITORS

Feeding SCHEDULE

NAME

NAME

NAME

Goals FOR TODAY

Questions TO ASK

Today's STATS

WEIGHT: LENGTH:

GESTATIONAL AGE:

LABS/MEDS/PROCEDURES:

WEIGHT: LENGTH:

GESTATIONAL AGE:

LABS/MEDS/PROCEDURES:

WEIGHT: LENGTH:

GESTATIONAL AGE:

LABS/MEDS/PROCEDURES:

TODAY'S *Nurse*

NOTES *& Reflections*

TODAY'S *Doctor*

TODAY'S *Weather*

Milestones

CURRENT *Events*

Positives

Hardships

Today... WE WERE BUSY!

FEEDING   READ   DIAPER

PHONE CALL   VIDEO CALL   ROCKED

SKIN ON SKIN   PRAYED   BATH

MASSAGE   TEMPERATURE   VISITORS

Feeding SCHEDULE

NAME	NAME	NAME

Goals FOR TODAY

Questions TO ASK

Today's STATS

WEIGHT: LENGTH:

GESTATIONAL AGE:

LABS/MEDS/PROCEDURES:

WEIGHT: LENGTH:

GESTATIONAL AGE:

LABS/MEDS/PROCEDURES:

WEIGHT: LENGTH:

GESTATIONAL AGE:

LABS/MEDS/PROCEDURES:

TODAY'S *Nurse*

TODAY'S *Doctor*

TODAY'S *Weather*

CURRENT *Events*

NOTES *& Reflections*

Milestones

Positives

Hardships

Today... WE WERE BUSY!

FEEDING	READ	DIAPER
PHONE CALL	VIDEO CALL	ROCKED
SKIN ON SKIN	PRAYED	BATH
MASSAGE	TEMPERATURE	VISITORS

Feeding SCHEDULE

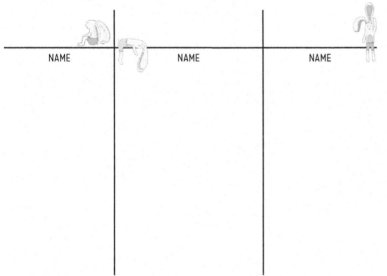

NAME   NAME   NAME

Goals FOR TODAY

Questions TO ASK

Today's STATS

 WEIGHT: LENGTH:

 GESTATIONAL AGE:

 LABS/MEDS/PROCEDURES:

 WEIGHT: LENGTH:

 GESTATIONAL AGE:

 LABS/MEDS/PROCEDURES:

 WEIGHT: LENGTH:

 GESTATIONAL AGE:

LABS/MEDS/PROCEDURES:

TODAY'S *Nurse*

TODAY'S *Doctor*

TODAY'S *Weather*

CURRENT *Events*

NOTES *& Reflections*

Milestones

Positives

Hardships

Today... WE WERE BUSY!

FEEDING

PHONE CALL

SKIN ON SKIN

MASSAGE

READ

VIDEO CALL

PRAYED

TEMPERATURE

DIAPER

ROCKED

BATH

VISITORS

Feeding SCHEDULE

NAME

NAME

NAME

Goals FOR TODAY

Questions TO ASK

Today's STATS

 WEIGHT: LENGTH:

 GESTATIONAL AGE:

 LABS/MEDS/PROCEDURES:

 WEIGHT: LENGTH:

 GESTATIONAL AGE:

LABS/MEDS/PROCEDURES:

 WEIGHT: LENGTH:

 GESTATIONAL AGE:

 LABS/MEDS/PROCEDURES:

TODAY'S *Nurse*

TODAY'S *Doctor*

TODAY'S *Weather*

CURRENT *Events*

NOTES *& Reflections*

Milestones

Positives

Hardships

Today... WE WERE BUSY!

FEEDING	READ	DIAPER
PHONE CALL	VIDEO CALL	ROCKED
SKIN ON SKIN	PRAYED	BATH
MASSAGE	TEMPERATURE	VISITORS

Feeding SCHEDULE

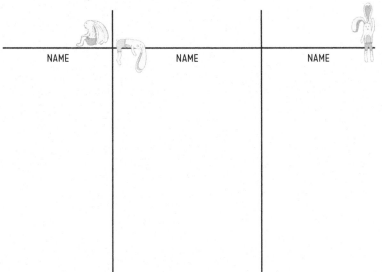

NAME   NAME   NAME

Goals FOR TODAY

Questions TO ASK

Today's STATS

 WEIGHT: LENGTH:

 GESTATIONAL AGE:

LABS/MEDS/PROCEDURES:

 WEIGHT: LENGTH:

 GESTATIONAL AGE:

 LABS/MEDS/PROCEDURES:

 WEIGHT: LENGTH:

 GESTATIONAL AGE:

 LABS/MEDS/PROCEDURES:

Photos

Weekly Recap

_____

_____

_____

_____

_____

_____

_____

TODAY'S *Nurse*

TODAY'S *Doctor*

TODAY'S *Weather*

CURRENT *Events*

NOTES & *Reflections*

_____
_____
_____
_____
_____

Milestones

_____
_____
_____
_____
_____

Positives

Hardships

Today... WE WERE BUSY!

FEEDING	READ	DIAPER
PHONE CALL	VIDEO CALL	ROCKED
SKIN ON SKIN	PRAYED	BATH
MASSAGE	TEMPERATURE	VISITORS

Feeding SCHEDULE

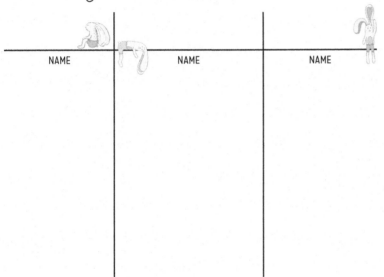

NAME   NAME   NAME

Goals FOR TODAY

Questions TO ASK

Today's STATS

 WEIGHT: LENGTH:

 GESTATIONAL AGE:

 LABS/MEDS/PROCEDURES:

 WEIGHT: LENGTH:

 GESTATIONAL AGE:

LABS/MEDS/PROCEDURES:

 WEIGHT: LENGTH:

 GESTATIONAL AGE:

 LABS/MEDS/PROCEDURES:

TODAY'S DATE: **NICU DAY #**

TODAY'S *Nurse*

TODAY'S *Doctor*

TODAY'S *Weather*

CURRENT *Events*

NOTES *& Reflections*

_____
_____
_____
_____
_____
_____
_____

Milestones

_____
_____
_____
_____
_____

Positives

Hardships

Today... WE WERE BUSY!

FEEDING   READ   DIAPER

PHONE CALL   VIDEO CALL   ROCKED

SKIN ON SKIN   PRAYED   BATH

MASSAGE   TEMPERATURE   VISITORS

Feeding SCHEDULE

NAME   NAME   NAME

Goals FOR TODAY

Questions TO ASK

Today's STATS

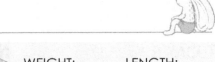

 WEIGHT: LENGTH:

 GESTATIONAL AGE:

 LABS/MEDS/PROCEDURES:

 WEIGHT: LENGTH:

 GESTATIONAL AGE:

LABS/MEDS/PROCEDURES:

 WEIGHT: LENGTH:

 GESTATIONAL AGE:

 LABS/MEDS/PROCEDURES:

TODAY'S *Nurse*

TODAY'S *Doctor*

TODAY'S *Weather*

CURRENT *Events*

NOTES & *Reflections*

_____

_____

_____

_____

_____

_____

Milestones

_____

_____

_____

_____

Positives

Hardships

Today... WE WERE BUSY!

FEEDING	READ	DIAPER
PHONE CALL	VIDEO CALL	ROCKED
SKIN ON SKIN	PRAYED	BATH
MASSAGE	TEMPERATURE	VISITORS

Feeding SCHEDULE

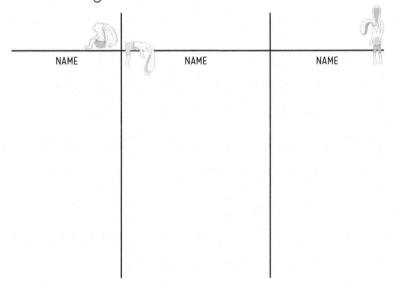

NAME   NAME   NAME

Goals FOR TODAY

Questions TO ASK

Today's STATS

 WEIGHT: LENGTH:

 GESTATIONAL AGE:

 LABS/MEDS/PROCEDURES:

 WEIGHT: LENGTH:

 GESTATIONAL AGE:

LABS/MEDS/PROCEDURES:

 WEIGHT: LENGTH:

 GESTATIONAL AGE:

 LABS/MEDS/PROCEDURES:

TODAY'S DATE: **NICU DAY #**

TODAY'S *Nurse*

NOTES *& Reflections*

_____
_____
_____
_____
_____

TODAY'S *Doctor*

_____
_____

TODAY'S *Weather*

Milestones

_____
_____
_____

CURRENT *Events*

_____
_____
_____
_____

Positives   *Hardships*

Today... WE WERE BUSY!

FEEDING

PHONE CALL

SKIN ON SKIN

MASSAGE

READ

VIDEO CALL

PRAYED

TEMPERATURE

DIAPER

ROCKED

BATH

VISITORS

Feeding SCHEDULE

NAME

NAME

NAME

Goals FOR TODAY

Questions TO ASK

Today's STATS

WEIGHT: LENGTH:

GESTATIONAL AGE:

LABS/MEDS/PROCEDURES:

WEIGHT: LENGTH:

GESTATIONAL AGE:

LABS/MEDS/PROCEDURES:

WEIGHT: LENGTH:

GESTATIONAL AGE:

LABS/MEDS/PROCEDURES:

TODAY'S DATE:　　　　　　　　　　　**NICU DAY #**

TODAY'S *Nurse*

NOTES *& Reflections*

_____

_____

_____

TODAY'S *Doctor*

_____

_____

_____

TODAY'S *Weather*

_____

Milestones

_____

_____

CURRENT *Events*

_____

_____

_____

Positives

Hardships

Today... WE WERE BUSY!

FEEDING	READ	DIAPER
PHONE CALL	VIDEO CALL	ROCKED
SKIN ON SKIN	PRAYED	BATH
MASSAGE	TEMPERATURE	VISITORS

Feeding SCHEDULE

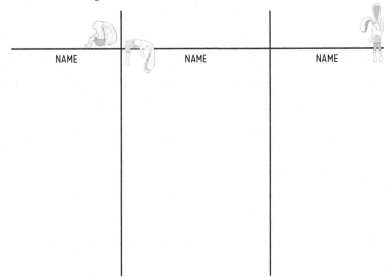

NAME   NAME   NAME

Goals FOR TODAY

Questions TO ASK

Today's STATS

 WEIGHT: LENGTH:

 GESTATIONAL AGE:

LABS/MEDS/PROCEDURES:

 WEIGHT: LENGTH:

 GESTATIONAL AGE:

LABS/MEDS/PROCEDURES:

 WEIGHT: LENGTH:

 GESTATIONAL AGE:

 LABS/MEDS/PROCEDURES:

TODAY'S *Nurse*

NOTES *& Reflections*

TODAY'S *Doctor*

TODAY'S *Weather*

Milestones

CURRENT *Events*

Positives

Hardships

Today... WE WERE BUSY!

FEEDING   READ   DIAPER

PHONE CALL   VIDEO CALL   ROCKED

SKIN ON SKIN   PRAYED   BATH

MASSAGE   TEMPERATURE   VISITORS

Feeding SCHEDULE

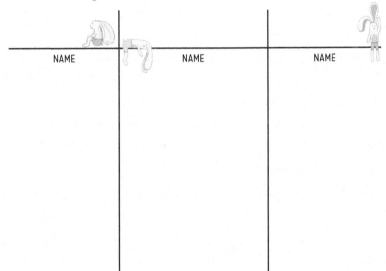

NAME	NAME	NAME

Goals FOR TODAY

Questions TO ASK

Today's STATS

 WEIGHT: LENGTH:

 GESTATIONAL AGE:

 LABS/MEDS/PROCEDURES:

 WEIGHT: LENGTH:

 GESTATIONAL AGE:

LABS/MEDS/PROCEDURES:

 WEIGHT: LENGTH:

 GESTATIONAL AGE:

 LABS/MEDS/PROCEDURES:

TODAY'S *Nurse*

NOTES & *Reflections*

TODAY'S *Doctor*

TODAY'S *Weather*

Milestones

CURRENT *Events*

Positives

Hardships

Today... WE WERE BUSY!

FEEDING   READ   DIAPER

PHONE CALL   VIDEO CALL   ROCKED

SKIN ON SKIN   PRAYED   BATH

MASSAGE   TEMPERATURE   VISITORS

Feeding SCHEDULE

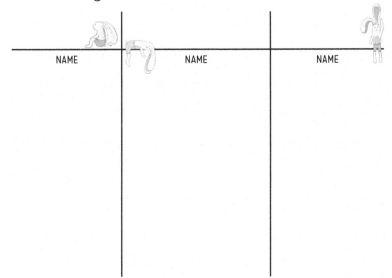

NAME   NAME   NAME

Goals FOR TODAY

Questions TO ASK

Today's STATS

 WEIGHT: LENGTH:

 GESTATIONAL AGE:

 LABS/MEDS/PROCEDURES:

 WEIGHT: LENGTH:

 GESTATIONAL AGE:

 LABS/MEDS/PROCEDURES:

 WEIGHT: LENGTH:

 GESTATIONAL AGE:

 LABS/MEDS/PROCEDURES:

Photos

Weekly Recap

_____

_____

_____

_____

_____

_____

_____

_____

TODAY'S DATE: **NICU DAY #**

TODAY'S *Nurse*

TODAY'S *Doctor*

TODAY'S *Weather*

CURRENT *Events*

NOTES & *Reflections*

Milestones

Positives

Hardships

Today... WE WERE BUSY!

___ FEEDING	___ READ	___ DIAPER
___ PHONE CALL	___ VIDEO CALL	___ ROCKED
___ SKIN ON SKIN	___ PRAYED	___ BATH
___ MASSAGE	___ TEMPERATURE	___ VISITORS
___	___	

Feeding SCHEDULE

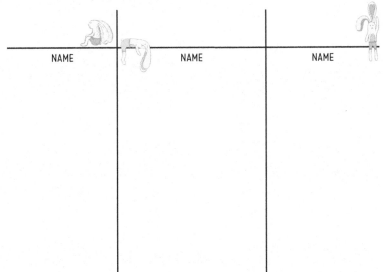

NAME   NAME   NAME

Goals FOR TODAY

Questions TO ASK

Today's STATS

 WEIGHT: LENGTH:

 GESTATIONAL AGE:

LABS/MEDS/PROCEDURES:

 WEIGHT: LENGTH:

 GESTATIONAL AGE:

LABS/MEDS/PROCEDURES:

 WEIGHT: LENGTH:

 GESTATIONAL AGE:

 LABS/MEDS/PROCEDURES:

TODAY'S *Nurse*

NOTES *& Reflections*

_____
_____
_____
_____

TODAY'S *Doctor*

_____
_____
_____
_____

TODAY'S *Weather*

Milestones

_____
_____

CURRENT *Events*

_____
_____
_____

Positives   *Hardships*

Today... WE WERE BUSY!

___ FEEDING	___ READ	___ DIAPER
___ PHONE CALL	___ VIDEO CALL	___ ROCKED
___ SKIN ON SKIN	___ PRAYED	___ BATH
___ MASSAGE	___ TEMPERATURE	___ VISITORS

Feeding SCHEDULE

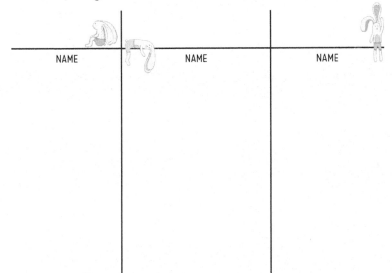

NAME _____ NAME _____ NAME _____

Goals FOR TODAY

Questions TO ASK

Today's STATS

_____

 WEIGHT: LENGTH:

 GESTATIONAL AGE:

 LABS/MEDS/PROCEDURES:

_____

 WEIGHT: LENGTH:

GESTATIONAL AGE:

 LABS/MEDS/PROCEDURES:

_____

 WEIGHT: LENGTH:

 GESTATIONAL AGE:

 LABS/MEDS/PROCEDURES:

TODAY'S *Nurse*

TODAY'S *Doctor*

TODAY'S *Weather*

CURRENT *Events*

NOTES *& Reflections*

Milestones

Positives

Hardships

Today... WE WERE BUSY!

FEEDING   READ   DIAPER

_____   _____   _____

PHONE CALL   VIDEO CALL   ROCKED

_____   _____   _____

SKIN ON SKIN   PRAYED   BATH

_____   _____   _____

MASSAGE   TEMPERATURE   VISITORS

_____   _____   _____

_____   _____

Feeding SCHEDULE

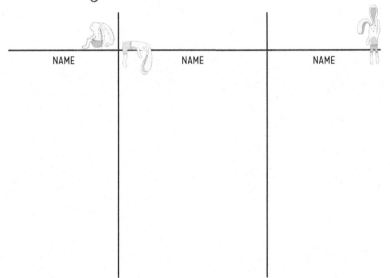

NAME   NAME   NAME

Goals FOR TODAY

Questions TO ASK

 WEIGHT: LENGTH:

 GESTATIONAL AGE:

LABS/MEDS/PROCEDURES:

 WEIGHT: LENGTH:

 GESTATIONAL AGE:

 LABS/MEDS/PROCEDURES:

 WEIGHT: LENGTH:

 GESTATIONAL AGE:

 LABS/MEDS/PROCEDURES:

TODAY'S DATE: **NICU DAY #**

TODAY'S *Nurse*

NOTES *& Reflections*

_____

_____

_____

TODAY'S *Doctor*

_____

_____

_____

_____

TODAY'S *Weather*

_____

Milestones

_____

_____

CURRENT *Events*

_____

_____

_____

Positives

Hardships

Today... WE WERE BUSY!

FEEDING   READ   DIAPER

PHONE CALL   VIDEO CALL   ROCKED

SKIN ON SKIN   PRAYED   BATH

MASSAGE   TEMPERATURE   VISITORS

Feeding SCHEDULE

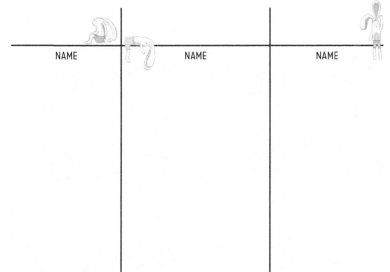

NAME   NAME   NAME

Goals FOR TODAY

Questions TO ASK

Today's STATS

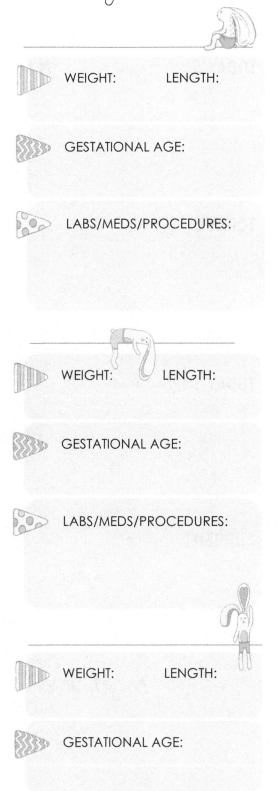

WEIGHT: LENGTH:

GESTATIONAL AGE:

LABS/MEDS/PROCEDURES:

WEIGHT: LENGTH:

GESTATIONAL AGE:

LABS/MEDS/PROCEDURES:

WEIGHT: LENGTH:

GESTATIONAL AGE:

LABS/MEDS/PROCEDURES:

TODAY'S *Nurse*

NOTES *& Reflections*

TODAY'S *Doctor*

TODAY'S *Weather*

Milestones

CURRENT *Events*

Positives

Hardships

Today... WE WERE BUSY!

FEEDING	READ	DIAPER
PHONE CALL	VIDEO CALL	ROCKED
SKIN ON SKIN	PRAYED	BATH
MASSAGE	TEMPERATURE	VISITORS

Feeding SCHEDULE

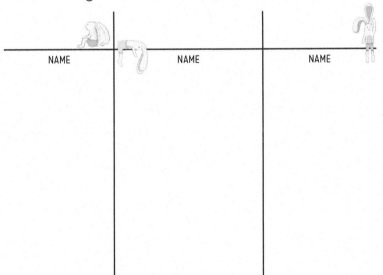

NAME   NAME   NAME

Goals FOR TODAY

Questions TO ASK

Today's STATS

 WEIGHT: LENGTH:

 GESTATIONAL AGE:

 LABS/MEDS/PROCEDURES:

 WEIGHT: LENGTH:

 GESTATIONAL AGE:

LABS/MEDS/PROCEDURES:

 WEIGHT: LENGTH:

 GESTATIONAL AGE:

 LABS/MEDS/PROCEDURES:

TODAY'S DATE: **NICU DAY #**

TODAY'S *Nurse*

NOTES *& Reflections*

_____

_____

_____

TODAY'S *Doctor*

_____

_____

_____

_____

TODAY'S *Weather*

_____

Milestones

_____

_____

CURRENT *Events*

_____

_____

_____

_____

Positives

Hardships

Today... WE WERE BUSY!

FEEDING	READ	DIAPER
PHONE CALL	VIDEO CALL	ROCKED
SKIN ON SKIN	PRAYED	BATH
MASSAGE	TEMPERATURE	VISITORS

Feeding SCHEDULE

NAME	NAME	NAME

Goals FOR TODAY

Questions TO ASK

Today's STATS

 WEIGHT: LENGTH:

 GESTATIONAL AGE:

 LABS/MEDS/PROCEDURES:

 WEIGHT: LENGTH:

 GESTATIONAL AGE:

LABS/MEDS/PROCEDURES:

 WEIGHT: LENGTH:

 GESTATIONAL AGE:

 LABS/MEDS/PROCEDURES:

TODAY'S *Nurse*

NOTES *& Reflections*

TODAY'S *Doctor*

TODAY'S *Weather*

Milestones

CURRENT *Events*

Positives

Hardships

Today... WE WERE BUSY!

FEEDING   READ   DIAPER

PHONE CALL   VIDEO CALL   ROCKED

SKIN ON SKIN   PRAYED   BATH

MASSAGE   TEMPERATURE   VISITORS

Feeding SCHEDULE

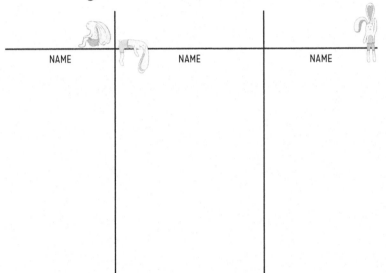

NAME	NAME	NAME

Goals FOR TODAY

Questions TO ASK

Today's STATS

 WEIGHT: LENGTH:

 GESTATIONAL AGE:

 LABS/MEDS/PROCEDURES:

 WEIGHT: LENGTH:

 GESTATIONAL AGE:

LABS/MEDS/PROCEDURES:

 WEIGHT: LENGTH:

 GESTATIONAL AGE:

 LABS/MEDS/PROCEDURES:

Photos

Weekly Recap

_____

_____

_____

_____

_____

_____

_____

_____

TODAY'S DATE: **NICU DAY #**

TODAY'S *Nurse*

TODAY'S *Doctor*

TODAY'S *Weather*

CURRENT *Events*

NOTES *& Reflections*

Milestones

Positives

Hardships

Today... WE WERE BUSY!

FEEDING	READ	DIAPER
PHONE CALL	VIDEO CALL	ROCKED
SKIN ON SKIN	PRAYED	BATH
MASSAGE	TEMPERATURE	VISITORS

Feeding SCHEDULE

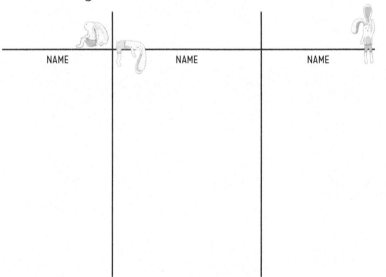

NAME   NAME   NAME

Goals FOR TODAY

Questions TO ASK

Today's STATS

 WEIGHT: LENGTH:

 GESTATIONAL AGE:

 LABS/MEDS/PROCEDURES:

 WEIGHT: LENGTH:

 GESTATIONAL AGE:

LABS/MEDS/PROCEDURES:

 WEIGHT: LENGTH:

 GESTATIONAL AGE:

 LABS/MEDS/PROCEDURES:

TODAY'S *Nurse*

TODAY'S *Doctor*

TODAY'S *Weather*

CURRENT *Events*

NOTES & *Reflections*

_____
_____
_____
_____
_____
_____
_____

Milestones

_____
_____
_____
_____
_____

Positives

Hardships

Today... WE WERE BUSY!

FEEDING	READ	DIAPER
PHONE CALL	VIDEO CALL	ROCKED
SKIN ON SKIN	PRAYED	BATH
MASSAGE	TEMPERATURE	VISITORS

Feeding SCHEDULE

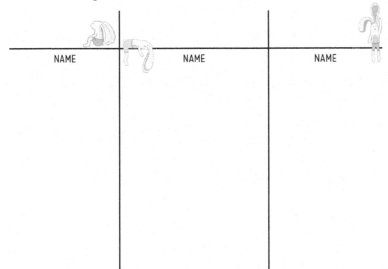

NAME   NAME   NAME

Goals FOR TODAY

Questions TO ASK

Today's STATS

 WEIGHT: LENGTH:

 GESTATIONAL AGE:

 LABS/MEDS/PROCEDURES:

 WEIGHT: LENGTH:

GESTATIONAL AGE:

 LABS/MEDS/PROCEDURES:

 WEIGHT: LENGTH:

 GESTATIONAL AGE:

 LABS/MEDS/PROCEDURES:

TODAY'S *Nurse*

NOTES *& Reflections*

_____

_____

_____

_____

TODAY'S *Doctor*

_____

_____

_____

_____

TODAY'S *Weather*

_____

Milestones

_____

_____

CURRENT *Events*

_____

_____

_____

Positives

Hardships

Today... WE WERE BUSY!

FEEDING	READ	DIAPER
PHONE CALL	VIDEO CALL	ROCKED
SKIN ON SKIN	PRAYED	BATH
MASSAGE	TEMPERATURE	VISITORS

Feeding SCHEDULE

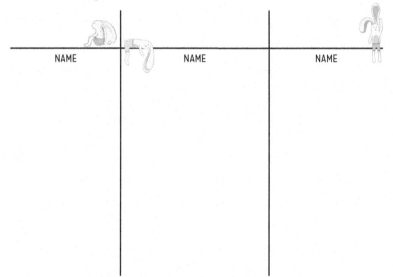

NAME	NAME	NAME

Goals FOR TODAY

Questions TO ASK

Today's STATS

 WEIGHT: LENGTH:

 GESTATIONAL AGE:

 LABS/MEDS/PROCEDURES:

 WEIGHT: LENGTH:

 GESTATIONAL AGE:

LABS/MEDS/PROCEDURES:

 WEIGHT: LENGTH:

 GESTATIONAL AGE:

 LABS/MEDS/PROCEDURES:

TODAY'S *Nurse*

TODAY'S *Doctor*

TODAY'S *Weather*

CURRENT *Events*

NOTES & *Reflections*

Milestones

Positives

Hardships

Today... WE WERE BUSY!

___ FEEDING	___ READ	___ DIAPER
___ PHONE CALL	___ VIDEO CALL	___ ROCKED
___ SKIN ON SKIN	___ PRAYED	___ BATH
___ MASSAGE	___ TEMPERATURE	___ VISITORS

___ ___

Feeding SCHEDULE

NAME   NAME   NAME

Goals FOR TODAY

Questions TO ASK

Today's STATS

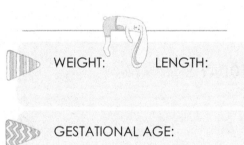

WEIGHT: LENGTH:

GESTATIONAL AGE:

LABS/MEDS/PROCEDURES:

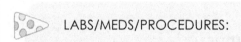

WEIGHT: LENGTH:

GESTATIONAL AGE:

LABS/MEDS/PROCEDURES:

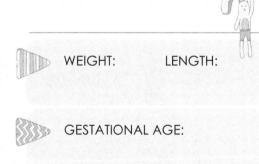

WEIGHT: LENGTH:

GESTATIONAL AGE:

LABS/MEDS/PROCEDURES:

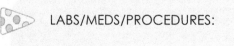

TODAY'S *Nurse*

NOTES *& Reflections*

_____
_____
_____
_____
_____

TODAY'S *Doctor*

_____
_____

TODAY'S *Weather*

Milestones

_____
_____
_____

CURRENT *Events*

_____
_____
_____

Positives

Hardships

Today... WE WERE BUSY!

FEEDING   READ   DIAPER

PHONE CALL   VIDEO CALL   ROCKED

SKIN ON SKIN PRAYED   BATH

MASSAGE   TEMPERATURE VISITORS

Feeding SCHEDULE

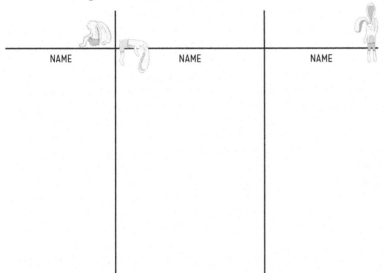

NAME   NAME   NAME

Goals FOR TODAY

Questions TO ASK

Today's STATS

WEIGHT: LENGTH:

GESTATIONAL AGE:

LABS/MEDS/PROCEDURES:

WEIGHT: LENGTH:

GESTATIONAL AGE:

LABS/MEDS/PROCEDURES:

WEIGHT: LENGTH:

GESTATIONAL AGE:

LABS/MEDS/PROCEDURES:

TODAY'S DATE: **NICU DAY #**

TODAY'S *Nurse*

TODAY'S *Doctor*

TODAY'S *Weather*

CURRENT *Events*

NOTES *& Reflections*

_____
_____
_____
_____
_____
_____

Milestones

_____
_____
_____
_____
_____

Positives

Hardships

Today... WE WERE BUSY!

FEEDING   READ   DIAPER

PHONE CALL   VIDEO CALL   ROCKED

SKIN ON SKIN   PRAYED   BATH

MASSAGE   TEMPERATURE   VISITORS

Feeding SCHEDULE

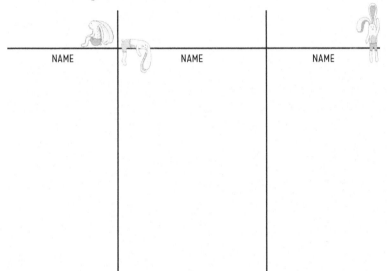

NAME   NAME   NAME

Goals FOR TODAY

Questions TO ASK

Today's STATS

 WEIGHT: LENGTH:

 GESTATIONAL AGE:

 LABS/MEDS/PROCEDURES:

 WEIGHT: LENGTH:

 GESTATIONAL AGE:

LABS/MEDS/PROCEDURES:

 WEIGHT: LENGTH:

 GESTATIONAL AGE:

 LABS/MEDS/PROCEDURES:

TODAY'S DATE: NICU DAY #

TODAY'S *Nurse*

TODAY'S *Doctor*

TODAY'S *Weather*

CURRENT *Events*

NOTES & *Reflections*

_____

_____

_____

_____

_____

Milestones

_____

_____

_____

_____

_____

Positives

Hardships

Today... WE WERE BUSY!

FEEDING   READ   DIAPER

PHONE CALL   VIDEO CALL   ROCKED

SKIN ON SKIN   PRAYED   BATH

MASSAGE   TEMPERATURE   VISITORS

Feeding SCHEDULE

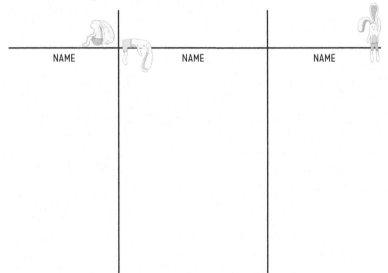

NAME   NAME   NAME

Goals FOR TODAY

Questions TO ASK

Today's STATS

 WEIGHT: LENGTH:

 GESTATIONAL AGE:

LABS/MEDS/PROCEDURES:

 WEIGHT: LENGTH:

 GESTATIONAL AGE:

 LABS/MEDS/PROCEDURES:

 WEIGHT: LENGTH:

 GESTATIONAL AGE:

 LABS/MEDS/PROCEDURES:

Weekly Recap

_____

_____

_____

_____

_____

_____

_____

_____

Going Home

NAME:
_____

DATE:
_____

GESTATIONAL AGE:
_____

WEIGHT & LENGTH:
_____

_____

NAME:
_____

DATE:
_____

GESTATIONAL AGE:
_____

WEIGHT & LENGTH:
_____

_____

NAME:
_____

DATE:
_____

GESTATIONAL AGE:
_____

WEIGHT & LENGTH:
_____

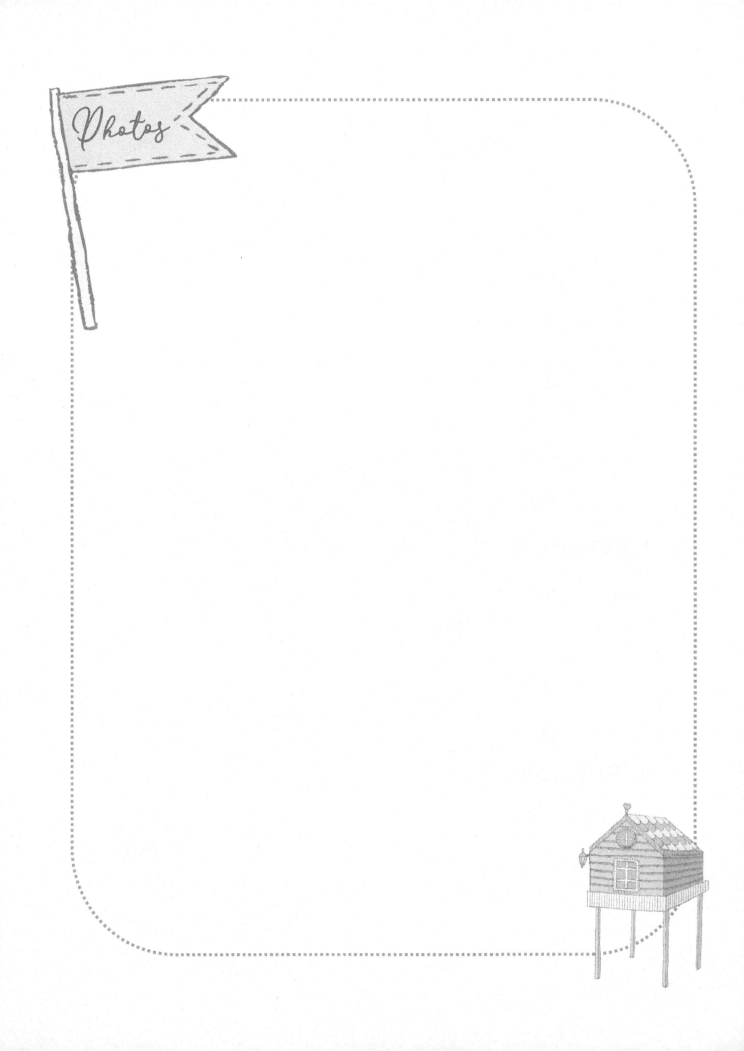

Photos

Photos

THINGS TO *Remember*

_____

_____

_____

_____

_____

_____

_____

_____

_____

_____

_____

_____

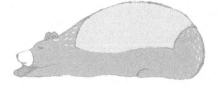

SOME CALL IT chaos WE CALL IT family